Just Hug a Bubble

Story by Phil Canalin

Illustrations by Ed Canalin

authorHOUSE®

AuthorHouse™
1663 Liberty Drive
Bloomington, IN 47403
www.authorhouse.com
Phone: 1 (800) 839-8640

Published by AuthorHouse 01/13/2015

ISBN: 978-1-4259-7453-4 (sc)
ISBN: 978-1-4969-6354-3 (hc)

Library of Congress Control Number: 2006909450

authorHOUSE®

dedications

To my three favorite hugs in the world....

Jessica – My inspiration for this story. At one-year-old you hugged everybody and everything in sight, including bubbles! You taught me that life and love expand when you have a family...

Kelsey – Wise beyond your years and too young to care! Your smile and heart are my sun and my moon…

Susan – As always, it is You, and forever will be.

…Phil

acknowledgements

This book wouldn't have happened without my brother, Ed, who used his great artistic vision and skill to illustrate what before I could only imagine in my head. Thanks, Ed! I sincerely appreciate April LeVay, from AuthorHouse, who supported me with care and knowledge. And I am grateful for Nanay and Tatay for teaching me to enjoy each day. A final thanks to teachers all over, especially Rosemary (Tarantino) Holmes, who take the time to help kids understand the joys of reading and writing, and many times send them on home with a hug.

The **Boy** was living in a Bubble. A big, bouncy, clear, unbreakable Bubble.

If you asked him, well, he couldn't remember how
this situation came to be. Just one day here was
this big, big Bubble and, the next thing he knew,

he was inside of it!

Now folks might say,
    "That Boy is stuck in that Bubble", or some,
    "the Kid is trapped in the Bubble." But not the Boy, oh no.
He loved being in that Bubble
        ...and
        he told everybody so.

"Ever since this Bubble and I got together...," he would
say, his hands pushing out playfully against the wall
of his Bubble,

"...I haven't been hungry
for food!"

And, "…The day this Bubble and I teamed up…,"
he'd sometimes tell, bouncing around inside there,
like a boy completely surrounded by trampolines,
"…I stopped feeling thirsty
for something to drink."

And, "With this Bubble all around me, why, I'm never cold. It's always warm and I feel just right."

He would boast to everybody, leaning against his clear, shiny Bubble, just like a billionaire leaning against his long, fancy, shiny car.

"I don't need anything, so I don't worry or need to work all day."
"I don't need to do a thing . . . just bounce around from place to place, wherever I want to go, just play and play and have a good time!"

One day, he happened to
make these same exact statements to a
little Girl. To his wonder, the
Girl started to cry. Why,
she was crying for him!
"How truly sad," she cried, shaking her
head slowly.
Tears rolled down from her eyes
and one hung at the tip of her nose. She leaned
her head tenderly against the Bubble,
letting it wipe the tear off.

"Sad?" he replied, patting her head gently, although his touch was separated from her face by the Bubble. "No way. No, I'm happy, really happy! I've got everything I need . . . the Bubble!"

"Happy you say? Everything you need?" she exclaimed, even more distraught. "But you can't touch anything or anybody except your Bubble . . . and nobody can touch you! Why, I feel so sorry for you I want to give you a hug right now, but I can't even do it . . . the Bubble's in the way. How can you live without hugs?"

The Boy's smile faded. "A hug," he said softly. "No hugs, forever and ever?" And he began to cry because he felt so alone, all alone in his Bubble.

The Girl was so terribly sad, but
she wanted dearly to comfort him.
Without thinking, not hesistating to consider
the Bubble that stretched out between them,
she reached to wipe away his tears.

Her hand
reached out . . .
and reached
through!

The Bubble popped, with just a whispered, "Pop."
She wiped away his tears and they hugged.

THE END

The Story behind *Just Hug a Bubble*

I was transitioning jobs to spend more time with my first daughter, Jessica, who had just turned two. Like many busy parents, I had missed Jessica's very first words and first steps while at the office working but I vowed not to let that happen again. With the somewhat nervous blessings of my wonderful and daring wife, Sue, I left my banking job of ten years, took a short sabbatical, re-immersing myself in my home life and family. One sunny spring day, Jessica and I were blowing big, beautiful soap bubbles in our backyard and she ran about, giggling and trying with all her might to catch one in her arms because she just wanted to hug a bubble. After many, many popped bubbles she became a bit frustrated. "I can't do it, Daddy," she told me sadly. I replied back, "I'm not sure you can hug a bubble, Jessie." But, showing the self-determination she would display often as she grew older and to this day, Jessica kept on trying. I simply continued blowing bubbles for her to chase and enjoying our moment in time together. Suddenly, with a beaming grin on her face and great joy in her eyes, Jessica carefully tiptoed up to me, a dazzling bubble gently cradled in her arms. She whispered, "See, Daddy, you CAN hug a bubble!" For a brief instant we were both so amazed and then, of course, it popped right in our faces! We laughed so happily and Jessica jumped into my arms and gave me a giant hug instead. I have always loved the idea that if you give a hug, you receive a hug in return. A hug is such a small thing, but, if given with true love and selfless caring, sharing a hug can be the greatest act of all. Don't be afraid to reach out to someone that needs a hug – it can mean the world to both of you.

Phil Canalin
Author

On sale now, Phil Canalin's.....

SLOW PITCH SOFTBALL – MORE THAN JUST A GAME

What is the secret of life and what does softball have to do with it?!

When William seeks his dad's advice, he is led on a marvelous journey that takes him to one important season in a lifetime of seasons for the adult recreation slow pitch softball team, the Willies. The stand-out league schedule includes pre-game festivities, game action, post-game barbeques and parties, all peppered with original song lyrics, softball-fare recipes, and some stuff you wish you just didn't know about your family. Players and friends fill the line-up card to take their cuts at retelling the complete team story. Like batters at the plate taking hacks against a junk-ball pitcher, readers will never guess the quirky directions the story takes them. But in the end, just like William, you'll find this is a tale of romance after all - a rollicking, nostalgic account of softball, family, and life. Slow pitch softball is more than just a game.

Look for Phil Canalin's newest publication, due out in January 2015.....

Invisible Society Fables

Cold.   Hungry.   Ignored.   Invisible.

2010: President Obama initiates his ten-year plan to end homelessness for all Americans. 2012: HUD estimates 637,000 people experience homelessness on any given night in the USA. Today: We're making progress...right? But the issue's not going away any time soon.

Invisible Society Fables looks at homelessness, using the storylines and morals of classic childhood fables and converting them to contemporary tales of homelessness in a straightforward, respectful manner. Let these new fables show the ironies and intricacies of circumstance while gently reminding us that anyone can be homeless - neighbors, friends, family, me, you. Most passersby choose to ignore the homeless person huddled on the curb, moving swiftly past, avoiding eye contact, literally side-stepping any connection. In the end, who seeks to hide and who becomes invisible?

ADVANCE REVIEWS for *INVISIBLE SOCIETY FABLES*:

"Phil Canalin's stories are heartfelt and real. They offer a glimpse into the realities of homelessness and illuminate the humanity of those who live it. This book is a must read for those who want to understand the experience of being homeless. Phil's stories and insights will also be invaluable and meaningful for the reader with more familiarity with homelessness and the people who live it."

Elizabeth Marlow, PhD, C-FNP
Executive Director & Co-Founder
The Gamble Institute - for parolees, by parolees
www.gambleinstitute.org

*"Phil Canalin's **Invisible Society Fables** captures the timeless lessons taught in classic fables of childhood but with a creative and valuable modern day twist. We see these lessons learned through the eyes of those many of us deem as invisible - the homeless. A heartwarming reminder of what keeps many of us as well as our homeless, individuals and families just like any of us, hopeful and resilient. These fables should be given to every child as a primer in teaching humanity, respect and compassion for others, no matter where they may come from, look like or where they live."*

Ravi Joshi
MS-I Healthcare Management
Harvard School of Public Health

Author Bio

In his spare time, Phil Canalin works in public health finance, recently for the noted Alameda County Health Care for the Homeless Program. He also loves to write fiction, short stories, poetry, and children's stories. Due for publishing in early 2015 (Divertir Publishing), *Invisible Society Fables* is his first short story collection based on his rare opportunities to observe, work with, and speak to homeless people and the dedicated people that serve and care for them. Phil's first published novel is titled *Slow Pitch Softball – More Than Just A Game* (Black Rose Writing, 2013). He also has collaborated on a cookbook project with his wife, Sue, *Dinner at the Sonneman's*. Phil resides in Alameda, CA with Sue, his high-school sweetheart and wife of 34 years. Daughters, Jessica and Kelsey, live in Hawaii and NorCal, respectively, both enviably facing the beach. Phil grew up loving *Aesop's Fables* and The Rocky and Bullwinkle Show's *Fractured Fairy Tales* and *Aesop & Son*.

Check out Phil, his BLOG and other writing projects at www.philcanalin.com and look for his next publication!

Author photo: Melissa Erikson